When I Was Nine
by James Stevenson

Greenwillow Books, New York

The illustrations are watercolor. The text type is ITC Bookman Light.

Library of Congress Cataloging-in-Publication Data
Stevenson, James, (date)   When I was nine.
Summary: James Stevenson remembers his family life during his ninth year,
particularly a summer car trip through several states in the West.
1. Stevenson, James, (date)—Biography—Youth—Juvenile literature.
2. Authors, American—20th century—Biography—Juvenile literature.
3. Illustrators—United States—Biography—Juvenile literature.
[1. Stevenson, James, (date). 2. Authors, American.
3. Illustrators]   I. Title.   PS3569.T4557Z478 1986   [92]   85-9777
ISBN 0-688-05942-2   ISBN 0-688-05943-0 (lib. bdg.)

*M*y own children are grown up now;
that's how old I am. But sometimes
I look back and I remember . . .

When I was nine, we lived on a street with big trees.

I had a bicycle, and I knew where
all the bumps were on the sidewalk.

We had a dog named Jocko.

Our telephone looked like this.
Our number was 3348.

My father had boots and a bugle
from when he was in the army
in the First World War,

and a mandolin from
when he was in school.

Sometimes when he came
home from work, he
would play taps
for us.

At night our mother would read to us.

CHUFF CHUFF

CHUFF CHUFF

We lived near
a railroad. Before
I went to sleep, I listened
to the steam locomotives.
The freight trains and
the express trains blew
their whistles as they went
racketing by in the dark.

In our backyard there was a beech tree. If you climbed high enough, you could see the Hudson River and smoke from the trains.

No teacher was ever able to teach me arithmetic.

After school I listened to the radio and
did homework. (There was no television.)

Bill, who lived next door, was my best friend. He was ten.
Bill was pretty good fun, but only about half the time.

HEY, BILL!
DO YOU WANT
TO DO
SOMETHING?

NOT RIGHT NOW.

When my brother had a friend over,
they wouldn't let me play.

I learned to pitch
by throwing a ball
against the garage door.

THUMP!

I skated on a pond in the winter.
The ice would crack with a tremendous booming noise.
But everybody said not to worry.

I put out a weekly newspaper.

I collected news from all the people on our block.

HOW I PRINTED THE NEIGHBORHOOD NEWS

1. I TOOK A CAN OF HEKTOGRAPH AND OPENED IT. HEKTOGRAPH WAS LIKE A THICK JELLY SOUP.

2. I DUMPED IT INTO A SAUCEPAN AND HEATED IT ON THE STOVE,

3. THEN POURED IT INTO A PAN AND LET IT COOL AND HARDEN.

4. MEANWHILE, I WROTE THE PAPER WITH A SPECIAL PURPLE PENCIL.

5. THEN I PUT THAT PAPER FACE-DOWN ON THE HARD JELLY AND RUBBED IT SMOOTH.

6. WHEN I PULLED OFF THE PAPER---

7.) --- THE NEIGHBORHOOD NEWS WAS WRITTEN ON THE JELLY BACKWARDS!

8.) THEN I PUT A CLEAN SHEET OF PAPER ON IT AND RUBBED, AND I GOT A COPY OF THE NEWS. I COULD MAKE LOTS OF COPIES.

Not everybody wanted one.

MR. FINERTY, WOULD YOU LIKE TO BUY A COPY OF THE NEIGHBORHOOD NEWS?

NOT RIGHT NOW.

Most summers my brother and I went to visit our
grandmother, who had a house near the beach.
We went swimming every day.

Grandma was a lot of fun. We would crawl into her room in the morning and hide under her bed.

Then we would pretend to be a funny radio program; she always acted surprised and she always laughed.

But this summer was different. In July we packed up
the car for a trip out west. A neighbor said he would
take care of Jocko. Bill and Tony waved goodbye.

We drove for days and days. My brother and I argued a lot. When it got too bad, our father stopped the car and made us throw a football for a while.

HERE···
CATCH !

NOT SO
HARD !

YOU SHOULD HAVE
CAUGHT THAT !

YOU THREW IT
OVER MY HEAD !

Then we got back in the car again.

At the end of each day we looked for a place to stay.
"What do we think?" my father would say.
"Plenty good enough," my mother would say.
And we would stop for the night.

My brother and I always wanted to stop and see
something special. Our parents usually wanted
to keep going. "Too touristy," they said.
But in Missouri we visited a big cave.

Our parents woke us up one night to look
at the sky. "What's happening?" I asked.
The sky was shimmering.
"It's the Northern Lights," said my mother.

On my birthday we stopped in a small town and
went into a store. My parents bought me exactly
what I always wanted . . . a cowboy hat.

At last we came to New Mexico.

We stayed at a ranch
and went on long, hot rides
into the mountains.

One day we rode to a waterfall. While the horses rested, we slid down the waterfall and plunged into an icy pool. We did it again and again.

It was the most fun I'd ever had.

We drove back home in August.
As we turned into our block,
Jocko ran to greet us.
It was great to get home.

Everything looked just the way it always had . . .
except maybe a littler smaller.

But I was probably a little bigger.
I wasn't nine any more.